A NOTE TO PARENTS

When your children are ready to "step into reading," giving them the right books—and lots of them—is as crucial as giving them the right food to eat. **Step into Reading Books** present exciting stories and information reinforced with lively, colorful illustrations that make learning to read fun, satisfying, and worthwhile. They are priced so that acquiring an entire library of them is affordable. And they are beginning readers with an important difference—they're written on four levels.

Step 1 Books, with their very large type and extremely simple vocabulary, have been created for the very youngest readers. **Step 2 Books** are both longer and slightly more difficult. **Step 3 Books,** written to mid-second-grade reading levels, are for the child who has acquired even greater reading skills. **Step 4 Books** offer exciting nonfiction for the increasingly proficient reader.

Children develop at different ages. **Step into Reading Books,** with their four levels of reading, are designed to help children become good—and interested—readers *faster.* The grade levels assigned to the four steps—preschool through grade 1 for Step 1, grades 1 through 3 for Step 2, grades 2 and 3 for Step 3, and grades 2 through 4 for Step 4—are intended only as guides. Some children move through all four steps very rapidly; others climb the steps over a period of several years. These books will help your child "step into reading" in style!

Copyright © 1991 Children's Television Workshop. Sesame Street puppet characters © 1991 Jim Henson Productions, Inc. All rights reserved. Printed in the U.S.A. Sesame Street and the Sesame Street sign are registered trademarks and service marks of Children's Television Workshop.

Library of Congress Cataloging-in-Publication Data
Ross, Katharine, 1950– Grover, Grover, come on over / by Katharine Ross. p.   cm. – (Step into reading. A step 1 book) Summary: With the help of his friends, Grover makes a kite. ISBN 0-679-81117-6 (pbk.)–ISBN 0-679-91117-0 (lib. bdg.) [1. Kites–Fiction. 2. Puppets–Fiction.] I. Title. II. Series: Step into reading. Step 1 book. PZ7.R719693Gr 1991 [E]–dc20   90-33947
CIP AC

Manufactured in the United States of America   10 9 8 7 6

STEP INTO READING is a trademark of Random House, Inc.

Step into Reading

Grover, Grover, Come On Over

By Katharine Ross
Illustrated by Tom Cooke

A Step 1 Book

Random House 🏠 New York

"Grover, Grover,
come on over
and help me!"
called Elmo.

Grover helped Elmo.

"May I have a newspaper, please?" asked Grover.

"Why?" asked Elmo.

"You will see!" said Grover.

"Grover, Grover,
come on over
and play with my kitten,"
said Betty Lou.

"Not now, Betty Lou,"
said Grover. "But may I
have some string, please?"

"Grover, Grover,
come on over
and plant a garden,"
said Ernie.

"Not now, Ernie,"
said Grover.
"But may I have two
sticks, please?"

"Why do you need
two sticks?"
asked Ernie.

"You will see!"
said Grover.

"Do you need
my string yet?"
Betty Lou asked.

"Not yet," said Grover.

"Grover, Grover,

come on over," said Bert.

"Let's make some pictures."

"Later, Bert,"
said Grover.
"But may I use
your paste, please?"

Bert helped paste
the two sticks
to the newspaper.

"Do you need
my string yet?"
Betty Lou asked.
"Not yet," said Grover.

"Grover, Grover,
come on over
and play at my house,"
said Herry Monster.

"Not now, Herry,"
said Grover.
"But may I have
some rags, please?"

"Why do you need
rags, Grover?" asked Herry.

"You will see!"
said Grover.

Grover tied the rags
to the bottom
of the newspaper.

"Now do you need
my string?"
asked Betty Lou.
"Not yet," said Grover.

"When will you need
my string?"
asked Betty Lou.

"Now, please!" said Grover.

"Right now!"

Grover tied

Betty Lou's string

to the newspaper shape.

Everybody helped.

"Thank you, everybody!"

said Grover.

Then Grover's friends
ran off to the park.
"Grover, Grover,
come on over!"
they called.

"OK, everybody!
HERE I COME!"
cried Grover.

"I am flying our beautiful kite!"